GETTING WITH THE GHOUL

SEXY SLEEPY HOLLOW BOOK 2

MOLLY LIKOVICH

For my mom.
Thank you for carrying me all these years.

I might enjoy being an albatross, being able to glide for days and daydream for hundreds of miles along the thermals. And then being able to hang like an affliction round some people's necks.
    -Seamus Heaney

So, Lydia, don't end yourself, defend yourself.
    -Beetlejuice The Musical

WHAT'S HAPPENED
SO FAR?

In book one of the Sexy Sleepy Hollow universe "Riding The Headless Horseman" we meet Arletta Harrington, a brash, snarky, angry young witch, specializing in divination. She's an outcast from the town due to false rumors created by her abusive ex about how she practices dark magic and shouldn't be trusted.

On Halloween night, while out on a walk, Arletta is abducted by the Headless Horseman, a creature she firmly believes to be just a myth. He whisks her away to his bone manor in the realm of the dead and they share a passionate night together. She learns the reason he doesn't have a head is because he was hanged for witchcraft when he was alive, and the townspeople back then would also behead witch trial victims. Arletta returns to the mortal world to hunt down his head for him. With the help of her new friend and fellow witch Samantha, the two are able to locate the hidden mass grave of witch trial victims. Arletta successfully returns his head to him and the two live happily ever after. In the companion short story "Smashing Pumpkins" found in the special edition of Riding The Headless Horseman we learn that when the Horseman (Hesse) was alive, he went by the name of Ichabod Crane.

AUTHOR'S NOTE

This novella, like its predecessor *Riding The Headless Horseman*, takes place in the Sexy Sleepy Hollow universe. This is a completely fictional version of Sleepy Hollow, New York and should in no way be compared to the actual town and its residents. This story also contains content intended for readers 18+ including mentions of past abuse, explicit sexual scenes, and suicidal ideation.

PLAYLIST

Achilles Come Down - Gang of Youths
The Albatross - Taylor Swift
The Archer - Taylor Swift
burn ur house down - emily jeffri
Burn Alive - The Last Dinner Party
Call Me Al - Paul Simon
Cassandra - Taylor Swift
Coffee In The Morning - The Stolen Sweets
The Good Witch - Maisie Peters
Heaven Is Here - Florence + The Machine
I Hate It Here - Taylor Swift
Insane (1920) - Black Gryphon & Baasik
the lakes (original version) - taylor swift
mad woman - taylor swift
Me & My Dog - boygenius
Not Strong Enough - boygenius
Pagan Poetry - Björk
Portrait of a Dead Girl - The Last Dinner Party
Robin - Taylor Swift
Say My Name - Beetlejuice The Musical

sex with your ghost - emily jeffri
"These Streets - Bastille
This Is Halloween - Izzy Reign
this is me trying - taylor swift
Weight of Living, Pt.1 - Bastille
Who's Afraid of Little Old Me - Taylor Swift
Worst Case Kid - Tommy Lefroy
You're So Dark - Arctic Monkeys
You're Dead - Norma Tanega

CHAPTER 1

LEAP FROM THE GALLOWS

Arletta Harrington is the loudest dead girl I've ever met. I see her everywhere, from the cracked spines of the cheesy gothic romance novels at the bookshop, to every tarot card I flip over late at night when I'm all alone. I see her over half-full glasses of wine across from an empty chair; the only guest at my table these days is her ghost. One can only endure a screaming silence for so long before one goes mad.

I suppose opening a portal of communication at her grave didn't help me maintain my sanity. At first I was worried the portal would drain her power, but Arletta, as I have learned since she moved away (saying 'moved away' makes it sound like she got an apartment in Manhattan and is living it up when she's ironically doing quite the opposite), is far more powerful than I or anyone else in town ever gave her credit for.

Everyone knew her as a seer or diviner and not much else, if they even believed in that stuff at all. Most people liked to view her as a bitch, a shrew, a slut, all thanks to that dickhead Ethan (that waste of space, pathetic excuse for a human being).

I'm proud to say I never fell prey to his lies about her.

I always admired her.

Even now.

On the third Halloween in a row that Arletta didn't knock on my door I went to her grave and found a letter lying there. It was sealed with wax, still warm, an emblem of a Jack-O-Lantern sunk into its gooey, maroon surface.

Of course.

I read the incantation and then a misty sort of hologram of her appeared above the tombstone. Like Sirius Black's head in the fireplace meets FaceTime. It was nice to have her with me, even for a little while, even like this.

But she rarely answers the incantation anymore.

I hope everything's alright.

Legends of her Hesse rage on in the Hollow, same as always. After she was absent two years in a row and presumed dead the legend shifted a bit to include the tale of a maiden dressed all in black riding alongside the Headless Horseman, a siren-like reaper of souls.

My friend may be all but dead to me, but the legend of Arletta Harrington lives on.

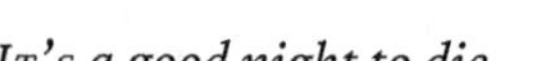

It's a good night to die.

The wind whistles through the air; it feels cleansing, as if the earth is ready to welcome me into its arms. I consider my suicide note; I wrote so many drafts of it, which was silly, it's not like the cops who find my dead body are going to care about my poetic blending of Emily Dickinson quotes and Taylor Swift lyrics. But the suicide note I left on Arletta's grave was more candid.

I hate it here.

I'm so lonely it hurts.

I wasn't built happy, and I don't know how to be happy. I was already hanging on by a thread the Halloween I found Arletta's tarot card in my bed. I was stupid enough to not fully comprehend the gravity of her decision to go back to the Horseman. I didn't realize it meant leaving me behind again to be haunted by the memories of the only true friendship I've ever had.

I helped her rob a hidden mass grave and she left me in this town to waste away.

Maybe this is an immature way out. Maybe wanting a way out at all is pathetic but my brain has rotted away to a point too emotional to process logic anymore.

I lean forward a bit, my fingers gripping the railing behind me tightly as the toes of my boots hang off the lip of concrete I'm perched on. The clock behind me will start chiming in a few minutes, I plan to be sprawled on the pavement below by then, dressed in my own beautiful blood.

"What a waste of a pretty face," a voice mutters from behind me.

I freeze. Contemplate. Maybe I've finally gone entirely mad and I'm hearing voices. It's one thing to hear voices at the grave of your not-dead friend through the magical portal she opened from another realm, but it's another thing entirely to hear them perched off the clocktower in the center of town in the middle of the night.

Especially a voice I don't recognize.

I decide that I'm not that crazy...*yet* and crane my neck over my shoulder to find the source of the voice.

There's a man sitting on the top of the steps leading up to the bell tower above the clock behind us. He has unnaturally red hair that sticks up in all places like he just rolled out of bed, which is a stark contrast to the suit he's wearing. It's a black suit so worn that it's more gray—a mere memory of black. His dress shirt underneath practically glitters in the moonlight like he's painted it in body glitter and he's smoking, a cigarette perched between unnaturally pale fingers and black painted nails, dark enough in a shade to make up for the sorry state of his suit.

He doesn't even seem to be paying me any mind, staring at the smoke billowing from the end of his cigarette like it's the most fascinating thing in the world. I'm suddenly really pissed off. Suicide is a private thing and here's this man coming in and invading the moment. I can't even off myself in peace in this goddamn town.

"Who the hell are you?" I demand.

The man's entire body seems to stiffen like he's been overcome by sudden rigor mortis. His eyes snap up to meet mine; they're a startling otherworldly green, demonic flames. I blink rapidly; maybe my lashes will brush away what must certainly be a hallucination, but there's no avail, the mystery man in the tattered suit remains behind me, staring at me with the most bewildered look on his face that's slowly morphing into one of...amusement?

"Can you see me?" he asks.

"Of course, I can see you."

The man's amused look splits open into a firecracker smile as he jumps to his feet. He tosses his still lit cigarette into the air, snaps his fingers, and it's gone.

Vanished.

What. The. Hell.

"Boy, am I glad to hear that!" He comes striding over to me. "This is my lucky day! And yours too it would seem!"

I grip the bannister tighter, leaning out a bit further over the pavement a world away below. "Don't come any closer! I'll let go!"

The man stops, hands out in front of him, he looks more like he's approaching a rabid dog he found starving on the side of the road instead of a depressed goth hanging off a clocktower.

"Hey, hey, I get it," he says.

I shake my head. "No, you don't. I don't even know you. Who the hell are you?"

"More important question is who the hell are you, babes, that you can see me." He smirks.

I bristle at the pet moniker of *babes*.

"Why do you keep saying that? What? Can no one else see you?"

He points a finger gun at me. "Bingo."

"Wh–what?"

He smirks wider. "Awe, doll, I already got you stammering?" He looks down at his still pointed finger pistol and pretends to shoot it. "Wait until you see what else I can do."

"Oh, for fuck's sake." I roll my eyes. "Go away, creep, I'm trying to focus here."

"On impaling yourself on that lamppost down there?"

I grit my teeth and try to ignore him, turning back to face the fate awaiting me below.

I hear footsteps on the concrete and before I've had time to process the continuing of his presence he's beside me, arms leaning over the railing I'm currently all but hanging from.

"I have an idea, babes—"

"Don't call me babes."

"How about instead of smashing up that pretty face of yours down there you...I don't know, say my name three times."

I turn my head slowly to look at him. The wind whips my hair back, making my eyes water, I blink away tears to take in the sight of him hunched over beside me, demonic flaming eyes beaming my way. He waggles his brows.

"What do ya say, darlin?"

"I don't even know your name." Is my totally logical response. "What even are you? A ghost?"

He shrugs. "Something like that."

"A demon?"

He nods. "Now you're getting it. Demon. Poltergeist. Ghoul. Spook. Thing That Goes Bump in the Night."

"Huge Fucking Pain in My Ass," I counter.

He smirks again. That goddamn smirk. "Well, it's hard to get a good look at it from here, babes, but I'm sure your ass is just lovely."

"Ugh." I look away from him again. Leave it to me to get haunted by the most perverted demon ever minutes before my untimely death.

"I have an easy name; you can guess it, and then you can say it, and we'll be good as gold, you and me."

"Why would I summon a demon?"

"Because...uh..."

I roll my eyes again. So, I'm being haunted by a perverted, *pathetic* demon. Great.

"Oh!" He snaps his fingers. "Because I can help ya!"

"Help me what?"

"Well...I'm sure you got your reasons for wanting to, ya know." He nods his head towards the ground below.

My fingers twitch, the wind blows, it's getting cold, and the railing is freezing to the touch. I don't know how much longer I can remain perched up here, barely hanging on. Sooner or later, for one reason or another, I'm going to have to let go.

"So, what if I do?" I say.

"I'm a demon, doll. If you summon me then I'll be at full charge and I can really help ya."

"I don't want your help. No one can help me." I look at the ground again with wind-watered eyes. My voice gets softer, almost lost on the wind. "Once I'm dead he'll be sorry."

I lean forward a bit, my fingers loosen their grip, I close my eyes, ready to welcome the abyss.

"Woah! No, no, no!"

I feel something brush across my chest, I open my eyes to see the demon has thrust his arm out in front of me, a pitiful attempt to try and keep me from plummeting to the earth.

"Whoever 'he' is won't be sorry, you'll just be dead."

I turn to meet his green-eyed gaze. His face is inches away from mine now, his scent invading my senses. He smells like a mixture of rich tobacco and damp earth. It's not revolting at all, I thought demons were supposed to smell like sulfur and rotting meat, but I guess I probably shouldn't be getting all my demon lore from *Supernatural* and *The Conjuring* franchise.

Arletta probably knows everything there is to know about demons.

She seemed to know everything about everything when it came to magic.

And all I seem to know about is herbs and nightmares.

The demon smiles, there's something devious in his eyes this time. "Why end your life when it seems to me some dickwad is the one who ruined it?"

"You don't get it," I say again.

"Come on, babes, say my name and I'll be on your team. I'll help ya take out whoever this mystery man is. An ex-lover, perhaps?"

His words ignite a fire in me. My fingers clench against the icy railing, and my nostrils flare.

"Woah, okay, relax, doll. Not a lover. Got it."

"You need to go away now."

"Come on." He bumps his shoulder playfully against mine like we're the best of friends. "It's easy."

"Fine, what's your name?"

"Well...I can't say it."

I groan.

"Listen, babes, I don't make the rules."

"Whose rules?"

He shrugs. "Hell if I know, the big baddie in the sky, maybe."

"*God*?"

He shrugs again. "Sure."

"How am I supposed to say your name if I don't know it and you can't tell me?"

He furrows his brows in what appears to be serious contemplation and for the second time tonight I wonder if I'm hallucinating. Leave it to my mind to make up the most absurd excuse for a demonic presence possible.

"Ah! I've got it!" His eyes glow with newfound excitement. "I'll give you a clue."

My fingers ache. I need to let go. Plus, the clock is going to chime soon, deafeningly loud. And this ghostly guy is so annoying. All signs point toward plummeting towards the earth.

And yet...

Something keeps me holding on, hearing him out.

Maybe I truly have gone mad.

"Fine," I grumble.

"Okay, a bird that flies over the ocean."

"A seagull."

"No, think poetry."

"Poetry?"

"Yeah, the thing with the lines that rhyme."

I want to smack him. "I know what poetry is, asshole."

He laughs. The sound is somehow taunting and melodic at the same time.

"I like ya, babes."

"That's great because I hate you."

He bumps my shoulder again and my fingers start to slip. My eyes widen as the crushing reality of impending death crashes down on me, strangling me like an...

The Albatross about my neck was hung.

I look at the demon again, eyes watering from the wind and unexpected fear as my hands begin to slip from the railing. It wasn't supposed to be this way. It was supposed to be my choice to let go. Why do all my choices keep getting taken from me?

His eyes flash vibrant verdant as he realizes what's happening. He thrusts his hand out to me and without thinking I grab on. My icy fingers clasp his chilled ones just as my feet scuff and slip against the concrete edge beneath me. I suck in a choked gasp of air as the clocktower's surface goes out from under me and suddenly I'm dangling in the air, a somehow corporeal ghoul, the only thing standing between me and death.

"Hold on," he says. "I've got you."

I struggle aimlessly trying to get my bearings. Tears wet my cheeks; shameful fear fills my chest. I reach up with my other hand to grab hold, latching onto his wrist, feeling the coarse fabric of his jacket beneath my frosted fingers.

"Look at me," he commands. I do. I let the blaze of his gaze swallow me up. "I've got you. I'm gonna pull you up but I can't do it by myself, you've got to help me. You can do it, alright?"

"Alright," I whisper.

He begins to pull, and I do my best to help distribute my weight. As I rise up my feet are able to meet the edge of the landing and I kick and scratch my way up and into his arms as he drags me over the railing. We crash down on the stone floor just as the clock chimes its death knell.

"Ah!"

"Fuck!"

We both go to cover our ears as the clock gongs on for a small eternity, rattling our eardrums. When it finally ceases and the quiet of the late night returns I'm able to fully register that I'm sprawled across his chest where he lays flat on the floor beneath me. I quickly roll off him, collapsing down beside him, the cold concrete surface seeping through the thin fabric of my dress, the tulle of my skirt and torn hem tangled around my muddy combat boots.

This isn't how tonight was supposed to go.

This isn't how it was supposed to end.

But it *was* supposed to end.

"Albatross," I breathe. I turn to face the demon to find he's already looking at me. Smiling. Of course he's fucking smiling. "Your name is Albatross."

"You can call me Al."

"Well, Al." I scramble to my feet as fast as I can and head towards the stairs. "Thanks for saving my life I guess."

"Thanks for letting me."

There's a tense static moment between us. I feel like I should say something else. I should do something else. But whether or not that's to stay and learn more about this specter or hurtle myself back over the railing and let all his efforts be for not, I ultimately decide on neither. Instead, I turn and run down the stairs as fast as I can, taking off for Arletta's cottage, never turning back.

CHAPTER 2

SOMETHING WICKED THIS WAY COMES

Let it hereby be known that I, Samantha Waverly Kos, am no stranger to death.

The thoughts plague me as I head home back to the only part of Arletta I have left; her house. She had written a will, unbeknownst to me, before vanishing with her lover's head that fateful Halloween night several years ago, and in it she left her worldly possessions to me. It made sense, we were both alone in the world.

There should always be a Witch of The Hollow she told me the last time I saw her. *There's power in being feared.*

I wasn't anything to be scared of though.

I wanted to be.

But I seemed to always fall short.

People revered and reviled Arletta, they just tolerate me. I sell my services same as her but making a living off of peddling herbal remedies in the age of big pharma isn't as lucrative as being a skilled diviner in a town full of anything but skeptics.

I round the corner onto Arletta's street. *My* street. I enter the house I've long since cleared out of most of the things she left behind; it was chilly, always living in her shadow. Every deck of cards or bowl of crystals left scattered about this place seemed to carry a spell cast by her, cursing me to get sick from the memories of what it was like to have her in my life, by my side.

I enter the house, expecting the sound of my chihuahua Annabel to greet me until I remember she passed away at the beginning of the month. One sorrow after another follows me in an ever growing storm cloud. I head to my altar in the back room Arletta used as her office, light a candle for Annabel, and before I know it I've collapsed to the floor sobbing.

"Well, aren't we dramatic?"

My head snaps up and I nearly scream.

Al is standing in the doorway to the office, leaning against the frame, smirking down at me.

I jump up and back up against the far wall. "What the hell! Get out of my house!"

"Awe, you're no fun."

"I'm serious, leave!"

He pretends to pick some lint off his sleeve. "No, I don't think I will." He looks around the room. "This place seems much more interesting than that old clocktower."

This cannot be happening. "How did you even get here? Aren't you like...tethered to haunt one place or something?"

He scoffs. "I ain't a regular, old ghost, babes. I go where I please. And right now that's here with you."

"Why?"

"Because your little stunt back there was the most entertaining thing I've experienced in years."

I just stare at him in disbelief. He looks as real as any living man; alright maybe he looks a bit more like the Lestat recast in *Queen of The Damned* but for the most part he looks like a normal, living person. The only truly spectral thing I've seen him do is vanish a cigarette and that could be a simple party trick. For all I know he's some weird cosplayer who stalked me home and broke into my house.

"How do I even know you're really a–a demon? You could just be some regular creep."

"Darlin, I'm an extraordinary creep."

And then he disappears into thin air.

A soft, undignified yelp escapes my lips as he vanishes from sight. I push off from the wall and spin in a frantic circle trying to locate him, but he's gone.

I don't think this is a simple parlor trick.

"Looking for little old me?"

I yelp again and look up to see him hovering above me.

He's *hovering*. Just levitating in midair.

"Shit," I mutter. "You really are a ghost."

He floats down to stand in front of me, and I'm able to register how tall he is. I barely come up to his shoulder (not saying much in comparison to the height Arletta boasts of Hesse having but here in the regular world six feet is impressive enough for us plebeians). His smoky-earthy scent wafts over me again as he moves in far too close for comfort.

"Demon, but same difference I suppose."

"And you're what? Here to haunt me?"

He shrugs, smirking. "If you like."

"I don't like. Get out."

He leans down a bit closer. "No."

I shove him.

I just *shoved* a literal demon.

He clearly wasn't expecting my physical outburst and I'm able to catch him off guard. By throwing my entire body weight against him I manage to make him stumble back a few steps.

"You're a feisty one," he says, amused.

"Why are you in my house?"

"Funny," he says, walking around the room. "I thought this joint belonged to that crazy witch. The white girl with the long, dark hair."

I cross my arms over my chest. "How do you know I'm not her?"

He glances back at me. "Well, for one thing, you're not white."

"I'm half white, asshole. Slovenian."

"Alright, *čarovnica*.*" Of course he would know Slovenian. "And what's the other half?"

"Mexican."

"Okay, and the witchy chick whose house we're in is as pale as the fucking moon with hair long enough to wear as a dress." He walks closer to me again. "You're a total knockout, don't get me wrong. Pretty brown skin, brown eyes, this silky-looking hair—" he reaches out and twirls a strand of my long brown hair around his finger, the loose curl wrapping itself against his ghostly skin. "—you're an absolute delight to look at. But you're not her. Of that I'm certain."

"Her name is Arletta Harrington."

My voice takes on a hollow, empty tone, her name clanging around against my teeth, painfully tugging on my vocal chords. No one mentions Arletta fondly, if they ever even mention her at all. Hearing Al recall her in his weird, factual way is oddly agonizing to endure.

---

*   Slovenian word for 'witch'

"Yes! That's right. I recognize the name now. So why ya in her house? You a squatter? This *is* her house, right?"

"Yes, this was Arletta's house. She left it to me."

I don't bother mentioning that Arletta is very much alive, just no longer *with* the living.

"I see. And who are you, babes?"

"Stop calling me babes."

He waggles his brows again. "Then give me something else to call you."

I sigh in defeat. "I'm Samantha Waverly Kos."

Al reaches out and boops my nose. "Cute name, babes."

"Ugh!" I storm past him and out of the room.

His laughter follows me along with the loud thud of his footsteps while he trails after me as I make my way into the bedroom and then to the adjoining bathroom. I slam the door shut in his face, clicking the lock into place. He knocks lightly.

"Locks don't really work on demons, darlin."

"I'm going to shower."

"Great, I'll join you."

"If you come in here I will fucking hex you."

"Oooo, I'm so scared."

I groan and let my forehead thud against the door. "Just don't come in here," I say softly. "Please."

I hear his footsteps retreating and the sound of his body flopping back on my bed, the old mattress springs creaking beneath him. There's a demon in my bed. Fantastic.

"Alright, babes, but only because you asked so sweetly."

I do my best to put him from my mind and hop in the shower. I let the hot water burn away at my skin, hoping it can wash away the emotional wreck of my failed evening. I almost reach a state of pseudo-relaxation when I notice a drastic drop in the room's temperature and see a shadow cross over the other side of the shower curtain.

"Al! Get out!"

"Whatttt," he whines petulantly. "It ain't like I'm looking at ya."

"You said you'd stay in the room."

I can't believe I'm arguing with a demon.

"So, why'd the infamous Arletta Harrington leave you her cottage?" he asks, completely ignoring my indignation.

I close my eyes, blocking out his shadow, and try to focus on the scent of my shampoo instead of the jovial tone of his voice as it moves around the small space. If words could dance, his would be doing a merry, little jig. My pomegranate and honey-scented shampoo invades my senses, dousing the remainder of the smoky earth Albatross left behind on my skin and I eagerly scrub it away.

"Babes?" Al prods.

"She's gone."

"And she didn't stick around to haunt this scene? Even with her bestie living here?"

I rinse the shampoo from my hair, reach for my conditioner, and consider telling him the truth. I'm the only living soul who knows what became of Arletta; I'd be deemed mad if I ever told anyone. I've kept this secret locked in a vault hidden deep in my heart, but my soul aches to share the truth of my friend's fate.

"Do you know the Headless Horseman?" I ask.

"Uh, not personally."

"No, like the legend."

He snorts. "This is Sleepy Hollow, babes."

"Well, he's real."

There's a moment of silence. *Great, even the demon thinks I'm crazy.*

"Okay," he says.

"Arletta's with him. In the realm between our world and the world of the dead, but *she's* not dead."

More silence greets me.

"I guess that sounds dumb," I mumble.

I rinse the conditioner and move onto body wash. I open my eyes and see Al's shadow leaning up against the wall at the edge of the shower curtain. I shrink back into the corner, but he doesn't make any moves to try and invade the space beyond the flimsy, plastic-y fabric separating us.

"Doesn't sound dumb to me, doll. Why's she there? He kidnap her?"

"Yeah, at first, but she fell in love with him."

Al snorts again. "That sounds healthy."

Well, their love is apparently so undying that she traversed back across the veil to dig up a hidden mass grave and retrieve his long lost head for him.

"Yeah, well, that's where she is. But even though she's still technically alive as far as I know, she's not coming back and she doesn't have any living immediate family to know the truth, so after a while she was declared dead."

"And you're the only one who knows?" he asks.

I nod to the shower wall. "I'm the only one who knows."

"Sounds lame."

I can't help it, I laugh. What an absurd response to my unbelievable confession, and to be coming from an other-worldly specter at that.

"Yeah," I admit. "That's one way to put it."

"Sooooo," he says. "How about you say my name, three times exactly."

"God, no. Why would I want to summon you? That

would just be unleashing pure chaos onto the unsuspecting citizens of Sleepy Hollow."

"Yes. Exactly." I see his shadow move closer to the edge of the shadow. "Wouldn't that just be swell, babes?"

"No, asshole. It wouldn't."

"Why not, doll? I can tell you want chaos."

"No, I don't."

He moves in so close his shadow blocks out almost all of the fluorescent light, casting nothing but the looming shape of him across the entirety of the shower. "Come on, darlin." His voice has taken on a more sinister tone. "You want it more than anyone in the world. I can tell."

I take a slow, deep breath, shivering from the chill emanating from him. Despite the heat of the water cascading over my skin I'm still covered in goosebumps. I part my lips to respond to his comment, but I can't seem to find any words. I should deny him. Chaos is dangerous and I avoid danger at all costs.

And yet...

Al huffs a laugh in the face of my stunned silence and then the scent of smoke fills the air.

"Hey!" The stench of tobacco brings me back to myself. "You can't smoke in my house!"

He groans dramatically. "Rules, rules, rules with you. Fine."

I hear him snap his fingers and the scent begins to dissipate. I open my mouth to thank him but then I notice his shadow melt away and the temperature goes back to normal, the hot water feeling scalding without his presence.

～

WHEN I LEAVE the shower and return to my bedroom Al is perched on the edge of my bed, studying the stack of books on my nightstand, most of them are old poetry books that belonged to my dad and a few books from work about different medicinal herbs. Something about seeing him like that, in my bed, eyes on my books, makes me feel more naked than I actually am under my towel.

I use this brief moment when his attention is distracted to dash to my dresser and grab an oversized t-shirt. I head back to the bathroom, but he jumps up and blocks my path to the door.

"What's the matter, babes? Dontcha trust me? We're all friends here."

I glare. "We are no such thing. You're an infestation."

He pantomimes being stabbed in the heart. "You wound me, darlin, I saved your life back there, you think you could show me some gratitude."

"I didn't *ask* you to save me."

"True." He leans one arm against the door frame, leering down at me. "But you certainly seemed to be holding on tight when you slipped. You know you could've just let go, dontcha, dollface?"

He sure likes to use a litany of pet names as opposed to just actually calling me 'Samantha' but at least he doesn't insist on calling me 'Sam' like so many people do.

And he's right.

I *could* have just let go.

That's what I wanted, wasn't it? To die. To finally put an end to this loneliness and seemingly ever-present pain. I've felt these phantom hauntings of depression and severe melancholia all my life but I relapsed into the darkest parts of myself ever since Arletta left, along with my only means of forgetting the painful memories she helped me repress.

I know I can't blame my mind's tricks on her but it's easier to do so.

I miss her and I hate her just the same.

I'm so desperate for company.

And here before me is Al. He's not the company I wanted, but he's company nonetheless.

That... still doesn't mean I want to change in front of him.

I keep my gaze locked on his as I move back towards my bed. Without removing my towel, I slip on my underwear and tug my shirt over my head. Once the fabric falls down above my knees I reach underneath and pull the towel away, bowing proudly.

Al claps dramatically. "Impressive, doll."

"I did ballet for ten years, I know how to change without taking anything off."

Al raises one eyebrow. "Ya did ballet? So, you're *flexible*?"

My smile drops and repulsion takes its place. "Alright, goodnight."

I hop into bed, burrow under the covers, and turn off the light. I can sense Al standing on the other side of the bed, my very own sleep paralysis demon, a personalized Imp of the Perverse.

"Dollface, how bout you read me a bedtime story?"

I ignore him. I feel the mattress shift under his weight as he climbs onto the bed, I scoot closer to the far side.

"Maybe I can give it a go," he murmurs softly, his voice sounding wistful. "It was many and many a year ago in a kingdom by the sea that a maiden there lived whom you may know by the name of Annabel Lee."

I grip the blanket tighter around me, his presence taking shape all around me. He sounds so pleased with himself.

Of course he would quote Poe.

"Yeah, yeah," I mumble. "I've heard this song before."

"Hmm." He creeps closer across the mattress. "Because I could not stop for death he kindly stopped for me."

Dickinson.

"The carriage held but just ourselves and immortality." I roll my eyes in the darkness. "Yeah, I know." I pull one hand out from under the covers and mimic turning a radio dial. "Next station."

I swear I can practically hear his smile as he slinks down right by me in bed, his head laying to rest on the pillow beside me. I inhale softly, my skin tingling just from the idea of his close proximity.

"But the two men, that last morning of death, before the first of light, watched the land of Venus it's sweetless shore, and thought—"

"This is the last of a man like me," I finish the line softly. "How do you know Anne Sexton? She seems to be a bit after your time."

"I'm full of surprises, babes."

"Whatever," I mumble. "Get off the bed."

"Ah, c'mon, darlin, don't be that way."

The mattress is suddenly devoid of his weight, and I realize why with a soft yelp when his levitating form appears before me, hovering in the air like a demented genie freshly jailbroken from their lamp.

"Pleaseeeeee, babes. I'll be good."

I peer up at him in the darkness from my blanket cocoon.

Don't trust him, is the repeating, raging thought.

But...

Arletta trusted a ghost-like being once. I judged her for it, silently, privately; I still do. But she's happy and I'm lonely and the haunting before me looks more and more tempting with every passing moment, especially as the nightly weight of *my* Annabel's absence blends together with the ever-present pain of losing Arletta…along with everything else.

"Fine," I grumble. "But don't hog the blanket."

I shift a bit, pushing the comforter on the other half of the bed back and Al swoops in delightedly, cozying up next to me. I turn away from him and suddenly feel his arm snake around my waist and pull me in close.

"Ugh!" I shove him off of me.

He chuckles. "What? If I can't hog the blanket then we're gonna need to conserve body heat."

"This is stupid," I grumble. "Do you even need to sleep?"

"No, but I can."

"Well, I *need* to. I have work in the morning."

He gasps. "And here you were going to kill yourself just to get outta ya shift?"

"Yeah," I deadpan. "I was going to call in dead. Go. To. *Sleep.*"

He laughs again but doesn't try to put his arm around me a second time.

"Goodnight, doll."

"Goodnight, Al."

CHAPTER 3

THE DEVIL YOU KNOW

*S*he looks like Snow White while she sleeps.

Someone told me that story a long time ago. I used to hear lots of stories. Lots of poetry. Lots of secrets. Lots of dreams.

She's not the first person to see me, just the first in a long, long, long time.

Time is a funny, tricky thing for me.

I can tell by her electric lights and the glowing phone on her nightstand that a great deal of it has passed. She's not even the first sad soul to tempt fate on top of the clocktower.

She doesn't seem to know that her Arletta Harrington went up there once, praying to a God or Ghost, or...something. Long before the night she disappeared into the mist.

I don't usually wish for the happiness of humans; they're vile things worthy of being defeated. I've only succeeded in possessing a few in my entire existence but what fun it was each time. I tried to possess the ever-reviled Arletta, but she was too strong a witch for my tricks. She couldn't see me, but she knew I was there.

She looked right at me.
Plenty of the living have looked at me.
Samantha saw me.

CHAPTER 4

OH, BOOOOOOOK

My alarm goes off and in my bleary, half-asleep state, I flop my arm out like a fish to shut it off. But I can't reach it. Something is blocking my path to the nightstand. I open my eyes and almost cry out in surprise.

Al is in my bed.

Right, of course, I let him crawl under the covers.

That's not why I'm surprised.

No, I'm surprised because at some point in the short course of sleeping hours I was able to salvage, him and I have ended up tangled around each other, a collection of intertwined limbs. My arm is draped across his torso and my legs are woven throughout his while one of his arms rests behind my neck and the other lands across my waist, his chilled fingers pressed against my hip. My t-shirt rode up while I slept to now feel his cool skin against mine.

My alarm beeps aggressively.

Al isn't breathing; his chest is completely still beneath my arm, but I guess he doesn't *need* to breathe.

I do my best to slip out from under him and shut off my

alarm. He doesn't stir. I grab some clothes and retreat to the bathroom to get changed, not wanting to risk it, he could be faking it for all I know just to get a peek.

When I re-emerge from the bathroom the demon's gone and I'm alone.

I refuse to acknowledge how disappointed I feel.

I'm going to be late for work.

So much for calling in dead.

"Morning!" Matilda calls out when I walk through the door to The Raven's Quill, the only decent occult-themed bookstore in town.

I'm balancing a to-go tray of coffees, a latte for her and a black coffee for me. I heave my satchel full of reading material for the day onto the back counter and set the coffee in front of my boss.

She takes her coffee from me but doesn't drink it. She gets up and goes to her back office where she stores her array of tea and coffee mugs to transfer the liquid. *I'm not a rat,* she always says. *I'm not going to consume anything out of papery trash.* I am not fazed by the papery trash of my to go cup and sip from it happily.

Matilda is probably the most effortlessly cool person I know. Witchy and wonderfully composed. Measured in a way Arletta never was, happy in a way I can never be. She's a kind boss, easy to talk to, amicable to work with. The only real qualm I have with her is she's friendly with Ethan...and my half brother. I don't think she ever truly believed Ethan's lies about Arletta, but the fact that she had the nerve to smile in Arletta's face and invite Ethan to parties behind her back never sit well with me. Arletta always said witches look out for each other; I'm not sure if Matilda really is a witch or just cosplaying as one for the aesthetic. I don't have the nerve to ask.

"So, it's book club night," Matilda says, walking back out to the counter, burgundy mug in hand. "Can you stay late? I have to take my niece to dance class."

"Sure." I'm never met Matilda's niece but she seems to always have dance class whenever there's an event in the store that Matilda doesn't want to be present for.

I hate book club night. A bunch of pretentious twenty-somethings cosplaying *The Secret History* sitting around nursing free coffee while discussing how deep Plato's *Symposium* is for the umpteenth time. We get it, 'call me by your name and I'll call you by mine,' same song and dance.

"What's the book tonight?" I ask Matilda.

She balances her coffee in one hand while tapping the passcode into the new iPad cash register with the other—her forearm, full of bracelets, jingles with each movement, a limb like a windchime.

"*The Odyssey.*"

"Ugh." I lean back against the counter. "They know there's been books published since the invention of the printing press, right?"

"Be sure to tell them that."

Matilda smiles at me again, her peach-glossed lips glimmering in the low lighting of the store. Her lavender hair is pulled back in a top knot, exposing her undercut. She always has a different pattern or shape shaved into it, this month it's a pentagram, fitting as Halloween rapidly approaches.

"Come on," she says. "Let's work on the displays."

The workday passes the same as any other day. Customers, cleaning, sorting. When the book club arrives after official closing time I set out their cheap coffee in flimsy water cooler cups and retreat to the back alcove of shelves, my safe haven—the poetry section. This is my favorite place to hide away from them.

I pluck a copy of *On The Bus With Rosa Parks* by Rita Dove and slide down onto the Persian rug, hand-stitched by Matilda herself. I blow the dust off of the old cover (not enough people purchase poetry these days). I start making my way through the book, muttering softly particular passages that speak to me. Halfway through I come across one that harpoons me in the gut.

> I was pirouette and flourish,
> I was filigree and flame.
> How could I count my blessings
> when I didn't know their names?

"You're so cliche."

I look up from the book to see Al hovering above me.

"Really, dollface, hiding in a dusty corner brooding over poetry while dressed like a funeral? It's so terribly macabre." He chuckles. "Strangely sexy though."

I, myself, am strange and unusual.

"What are you doing here?" I aggressively whisper.

"Uh, haunting you?"

I get up and peek around the shelves to ensure the book club hasn't noticed me talking to myself. Muttering poetry under my breath is one thing; having a full-on conversation with a specter is another.

Al comes up behind me, grabs my hips, and leads in close whispering in my ear. "Boo."

I clench my jaw, and spin around to look at him. He keeps his hands on my hips.

"Hey, babes, looking good." His hands lightly squeeze. "So, what'd ya say?"

"To what?"

"Duh." He rolls his eyes. "Summoning me. Come on, darlin, just say my name three times in a row, and I can really show you a good time. Help you get back at whoever it is that's got you looking so gloomy all the time."

He says 'all the time' like he's known me for ages, as if we're just two best friends spending yet another day together. It stirs something strange inside me that if I were a more mentally stable individual I might be able to fully process. But seeing as I'm post huge suicidal gesture, I don't think I'm quite there yet.

"Al, you can't be here." I press my hands flat against his chest but I don't push him away.

"Are you sore because I left ya all by your lonesome this morning?"

Yes.

"No. I wanted you gone then and I want you gone now."

"Mmhhm." He leans in close until his face is just a few inches from mine, his smoky breath thick in the air. "Then why'd you wrap yourself around me while you were sleeping?"

"I—" I have no good response. While it wasn't a conscious decision to snuggle with this ghoul it still shows I felt comfortable enough to do so. It shows I was lonely enough to do so. "Regardless, this is where I work. You can't haunt me here."

He groans like a child while levitating back above me

and doing a literal flip in the air. Really, how am I supposed to take him seriously when he behaves like this? He's the least intimidating poltergeist ever.

"You're no fun," he pouts.

"Would you just leave already? Everyone's going to think I'm insane if they hear me talking to you."

"You are insane. Or did you forget that less than twenty-four hours ago you were ready to toss yourself off the clocktower? Thank goodness you didn't." He grabs my face in his hand, fingers squishing my cheeks together as he comes to float almost horizontally in front of me. "Told ya I don't want you to waste this pretty face."

I smack his hand away. "Is that all I am to you? A pretty face?"

"Course not, darlin, you've also got quite a nice body."

I move my hand without thinking and raise it to slap him across the face, but he catches my wrist before my palm can make contact with his pale skin.

"Ah ah, what would the scholars out there think if they heard you hitting someone?"

I tug on my arm, but he won't release me. He pulls me closer.

"I'm teasing, babes. You're much more than just a pretty face."

With that he vanishes, leaving me alone with the dusty books and echoing voices going on and on about whether Penelope was *really* a victim.

God, I *hate* book club night.

CHAPTER 5

I AM NOT THERE, I DO NOT SLEEP

By the time the band of dark academia fetishists leave The Raven's Quill it's dark out and pouring rain. The pathetic fallacy seems to ben in full force tonight.

Luckily Matilda always has umbrellas laying around and on her person. She's never spotted out and about town without one. On sunny days she has elaborate lace parasols and on rainy or overcast days she has a variety of typical ones to stave off whatever the clouds have in store. I manage to find a plain black one in the back storage closet and head off.

My feet carry me to the cemetery without thinking. I pass Arletta's mock grave, noticing the suicide note I left there is gone, the rain probably turned it to mush. It's not like anyone would've taken it, no one visits her grave unless it's drunk teens on a dare. I keep walking deeper into the brush and brambles of the older, unkempt parts of the cemetery until I reach a large monument tombstone. I haven't visited in a while.

I had intended to see them soon.

Now who knows how long it will take.

I stand under the pouring rain, the hem of my floor-length dress soaked through several inches with mud, my boots squelching in the damp grass. I feel tears in my eyes and blink them away. Withered flowers are resting at the base of the grave, a half-melted lonely candle sitting atop it. I exhale slowly, and raise my hand out from under the cover of the umbrella until it hovers above the damp wick. I wave it across and the candle sputters to life, a tiny flame burning amidst the rain.

I sense Al's presence beside me before I hear his voice.

"Impressive work, babes. Got any other tricks?"

"I can manipulate things that have to do with the earth," I say. "Mostly herbs and plants but I can manage a candle or two." I flick my wrist and the wilted flowers perk up the tiniest bit. "Nothing much."

Al grunts his approval then studies the tombstone again. "Marko and Julia Kos. Those your folks?"

I nod. "Uh huh. My middle name Waverly was my mom's maiden name, there's a tradition on her side of the family of giving the maiden names to the daughters as middle names as a way to keep the lineage of women alive." I'm rambling, I doubt this demon cares about the history of my name.

"That's good," he says.

"Yeah," I mutter.

"How'd they die?"

"Car crash. I was sixteen."

"How old are ya now?"

I glance over at him, his usual mischievous, taunting expression is gone and something much more earnest has taken its place.

"I'm twenty-six."

He doesn't say anything to that, I suppose time doesn't mean the same thing to an eternal being like him. Ten years is nothing in the grand scheme of things, but it's everything to me.

"Do ya miss them?"

I sniff back more tears, rain drops slick on my cheeks. "Terribly."

"Huh."

I look at him again but he's not staring at me anymore, his eyes are on my parents' grave, studying it like it's a puzzle.

"Have you ever missed someone?" I ask.

He glances at me. "I think I'd miss you."

"You just met me."

He shrugs. "So?"

"But...what about your family? Your parents?"

He laughs softly. It doesn't sound cruel but almost sad.

"I'm a demon, doll, my folks ain't the same thing as yours. I've got a mom, I guess ya could call her that. She was what you humans would call a succubus that spawned me into existence and she made it *quite* clear all along that she never wanted me to exist."

"That's terrible," I whisper to the rain.

He shrugs again. His green eyes glow in the gloom of the night.

"Were you ever a child?" I ask him.

Al moves back a few steps and leans up against the grave across from my parents. He materializes a pre-lit cigarette and takes a drag, it remains undaunted by the rain. I realize Al does as well, the water seems to just slide off him without dampening a thing.

"Not really," he says around a smoky exhale. "I was

spawned and then I was sort of nebulous for a while. Just a shadowy idea, and then I was me."

I rest the umbrella's handle against my shoulder and go to join him, leaning against the grave.

"So you've always been this?" I gesture to his body.

He smirks around the smoke billowing out his mouth like a freight train. "Yeah, darlin, I've always been this."

I nod and look back at my parents' resting place. The candle flickers determinedly against the onslaught of rain. I feel cool skin against my face. Al's calloused fingers lightly grip my chin and turn my face towards him, tilting my head back. He's looking at me like I'm a painting in a museum he wants to study for hours. It's the way I've always wanted to be looked at; gazed upon like I'm something worth wanting.

His voice is soft and kind when he speaks. "Hey, babes."

"Hey, Al," I whisper back.

We hesitate a moment longer.

Then he pulls my face closer, leans down, and presses his mouth to mine.

It's a hesitant, gentle kiss at first. Two mouths trying to make sense of each other as they fit together for the first time, but soon we're overcome by the intense desire to be closer to each other. I let the umbrella fall away and the rain beat down on me as I stand on tip toe to wrap my arms around Al's neck. He follows suit, wrapping his around my waist as he presses at the seam of my lips with his tongue. I whimper softly, and I can tell the sound does something to him. His otherworldly body shudders slightly against mine and in one fluid motion he moves his hands from my waist to my legs, hooking them under the backs of my thighs and hoisting me up to sit on the tombstone. I don't stop to question how disrespectful it is to whatever dead is buried beneath us that I'm getting it on with a ghoul atop their eternal resting place, I'm drowning deep in the invasive feeling of Al's tongue flicking against my teeth, his fingers digging into my thighs, his smoky breath chilly against my skin.

"Albatross," I murmur without a second thought, his full demonic name slipping from my tongue.

He tears his mouth away from mine to kiss along my jaw and down my neck.

"Albatross," I say again, my voice breathy in the night air.

"Mmm. Say my name, babes."

"Al—"

Sense crashes into me like a semi-truck.

I move slowly, my limbs languid, my mind muddled. I push him away from me with as much strength as I can muster in my disoriented state. He's so preoccupied with pressing his lips to every inch of my throat that he doesn't have time to try and stop my shove. He stumbles back and I throw myself off the grave. I grip my muddy dress in my fists and take off for the cemetery entrance. Matilda's umbrella blown away in the wind; I'll apologize to her tomorrow.

"Babes, what the hell—"

I should keep walking. I should find a way to exorcize him along with all my other demons, the ones taking up space in my mind—in my *soul*. But I can't fight it; I need to scream at someone, I need to be angry at someone, and Al seems like the perfect target for such an outburst.

I turn around and face him through the sheets of rain separating us. "That was a horrible trick."

"What are you—" He seems to register the anguish and shame in my gaze. "Doll, that wasn't what I was trying to do."

I scoff. "Oh, sure. It's what you've wanted since you pulled me back onto the clocktower. I get it, I'm not the girl anyone actually cares about. I'm the girl you use, the girl you lie to, the girl you humiliate!" My words catch in my throat, the truth too scratchy and searing to speak. I drop my gaze, shaking my head as I stare at my muddy boots. "I'm being stupid. You're a demon. Of course you don't care about my feelings."

"I didn't say that."

My scoff turns into a hysterical laugh. When I manage to meet his stare again he looks truly perplexed by me. I don't blame him.

"*Do* you care, Al? Do you really care about the feelings of some sad, lonely human you just met?"

He's silent for a moment but then steps closer to me. My feet shift in the mud, I consider bolting, leaving this pain behind in the cemetery (except I can't because he can just follow me anywhere and no lock is heavy or thick enough to ever keep him out). Still, something in his fiery eyes keeps me rooted to the spot.

"Maybe I do."

"You don't," I insist. "No one does. Why do you think I want to die?" I wave my hand in the direction of my parents' grave. "Everyone who actually cares about me is gone."

Mom, Dad, Arletta.

Goddamn Arletta.

Why did you leave me here all alone?

I try to leave again, turning away from Al once more,

but he does what it hasn't occurred to me up until now to expect from him:

Something demonic.

He lunges after me, wraps one arm around my chest and clamps the other over my mouth as he drags me, kicking and flailing, back into the graveyard.

I can't believe this is how I'm going to die.

Maybe Arletta will be there to guide me from one realm to the next.

See you soon, Mom and Dad.

Something brushes against my face. I realize it's the branches of the willow tree at the center of the cemetery. Al drags me beneath the cover of the willow, shielding me from the freezing rain. He spins me around and presses me up against the trunk, one hand still on my mouth, the other wrapped around my throat, a necklace of fingers.

"Don't tell me I don't care," he practically snarls.

I try to speak but his hand presses hard against my lips and I can't form a single coherent sound.

"If I remove my hand are you gonna scream or be a good girl?"

Fucking hell.

I still can't verbally answer him with his hand gag, so I hold his stare and do my best to convey through my eyes that I'll be quiet.

He sighs and removes his hand from my mouth but leaves the other around my neck. He's not squeezing hard enough to choke but the pressure is too present to ignore.

"Why would you care about me?" I ask. "I'm no one."

"I don't know," he admits. "I saw you up there, and when I realized you could see me I just..." his fingers twitch around my throat, pressing down a bit too hard. I gasp softly. He doesn't remove his hand, and I don't ask him to.

"Just what?"

"You just looked like somebody I could relate to."

"Al, you're a demon."

"Yup. And you're suicidal."

"That doesn't mean I'm crazy."

He leans over me, dropping his free hand to my hip, and pressing me further into the tree, the bark scraping against my soaked dress.

"Maybe, maybe not," he says.

I glance down at his hand where it's doing its best to bruise through my dress.

"Let me go, Al."

"You're not walking away from me again, doll."

"Well, I'm not summoning you."

"Once again, babes, I wasn't trying to get you too." This time he does squeeze my throat on purpose—*hard*. I gasp, eyes widening in fear, he just laughs at me. It's so sick and condescending. "Oh no, is poor little Samantha scared of the Big Bad Ghost?"

He never seems to want to call me Samantha so hearing him use it now hurts, I never knew my own name could feel so demeaning.

"I hate you," I rasp against his chokehold.

He grins lecherously. "You don't though. And you hate *that*. But face it, babes—" he moves in so close that all it would take is one slight shift to press my mouth to his again. "—you like that you can see me."

"I—"

He squeezes my throat again and I gasp.

"Don't lie, darlin."

"Fine," I breathe, his hand loosens a bit. "I don't hate you." His fingers provide a bit more slack, it becomes easier to breathe but he still doesn't fully release me. "But right now you're pissing me the fuck off. I came here to be..."

Why did I come here? To visit my parents? Yes. Part of me still wishes I had succeeded last night and was with them now. But a bigger, stronger, louder part of me is grateful Al was there to pull me back—to save me. And I hate being saved, I hate that I needed saving and didn't even know it.

Al's hand releases my throat and his thumb brushes against my cheek. It takes me a moment to realize he's brushing away a tear.

"You're so sad," he murmurs.

I wipe at my face as he snakes his hand around to cup the back of my head. I don't make any moves to stop him from doing so. It feels so good to be held even by a beast as cruel as him.

"I understand," he says.

"No, you don't. You've never lost anyone. Lost *anything.*" I press my hand to his chest, and inhale softly at the silence beneath his skin. Of course his body is devoid of a beating heart. "Do you even know what it feels like to love, Al? Do you even have a heart to break?"

He holds my gaze like a wild sea tossing a sailboat about. I'm about to fall overboard.

"I can feel, babes. Ain't that enough?"

"Enough for what?"

His fingers tighten the slightest bit in my hair. "For *you.*"

"I don't understand what you want from me," I say softly. "I won't summon you. I don't want that kind of chaos, no matter what you think."

He smirks. "You're a bad liar, Samantha Kos."

"You're a bad person, Albatross."

"Then shoot me down."

I move my hand from his silent heart to rest against his neck, my fingers too small to even come close to encapsulating his throat. What do you call a portent around the neck of the Albatross itself?

Me.

"I can't," I whisper. He shifts forward and rests his forehead against mine. "You've come to destroy me."

"Mmm." He grazes his nose along mine. "Maybe. But what a wonderful way to go."

His mouth finds mine again.

I part my lips; whether to protest, whimper, or beg, I don't know. He takes advantage of it though, plunging his tongue deep into my mouth and tangling it with my own. I give into his touch once again, tilting my hips further against his hand, shifting to press my chest against his, savoring the way his body feels up against mine. He keeps one hand cradling my head while the other skims across my stomach, dancing dangerously close to my center.

He tugs lightly on my dress. "Move this," he breathes against my lips.

I hesitate. Even with my rain-soaked dress between us I still feel aflame from his hands on me. It seems like it's been an eternity since someone's physical attentions didn't make me cringe and feel like ants were parading up and down the surface of my skin.

"I won't hurt you," Al whispers.

I scoff and lean my head back against the tree to meet his eyes, making sure my bruised throat is on full display for him.

I watch his eyes trail along my neck to where the outline of his hand is splayed across my skin, he chuckles, leaning in close again. "Alright, babes. I won't hurt you *again*."

I let go of any remaining sanity I might have had left.

I let my eyes flutter closed and begin to lift up my long dress, bunching the fabric in my hands until the hem crests above my knees, smearing mud slick against my chilled thighs. Al slides his hand up my leg, fingers tracing shapes across my upper thigh. I inhale, registering that they're not shapes, they're letters.

MINE

I part my lips in a smile, it's almost laughable that I would get felt up by a demon under the old willow tree in the haunted cemetery. The sad girl meets a tragic fate in the end one way or another. But when his crafty fingers find my center, gliding over the fabric of my underwear—soaked from something other than the rain—nothing about this feels tragic.

Al's lips meet mine again, swallowing the soft moan building in my throat. The pads of his fingers circle my clit over the thin layer of damp panties slick between my thighs as my arms grip at the lapels of his tattered jacket. We break apart from our kiss, moans falling like diamonds from my mouth, Al chuckles at the sound, pushes aside my underwear and inserts two fingers inside me. I moan louder, and let my pleasure wake the dead. He begins to pump his digits against me, dragging embarrassing whimpers and whines from deep in my lungs, exasperating me to the point that all I can muster is letting my head fall back against the willow's sturdy trunk once more and get lost in the feel of his fingers inside me. He crooks them forward inside me to press against my inner wall, hitting the spot that makes lucky women see stars. I almost forgot the feeling of pleasure at someone else's hands. Most men don't care at all if the woman has a good time; they operate off of years of being told they're hitting all the right spots when in actuality they're nowhere near them, and in the end they're still rewarded with a well-crafted fake orgasm.

Al clearly will not settle for the mediocrity of a mortal man when it comes to how his fingers move inside me. I whimper louder and tilt my hips closer, practically entirely on top of his hand now, I need him deeper inside me, I need the thrusts harder, I need to be fuller. I want to get drunk off this feeling and go mad from his touch.

He descends on my neck, toying with the sensitive skin beneath my ear, blowing hot, smoky air against my face, tantalizing me with his heady, earthy scent. I part my lips to moan his name but stop myself, worried about what will happen if I let myself get carried away with that again. Al seems to sense my hesitation and laughs.

"Don't worry, darlin, I won't hold it against ya."

Then he presses the full weight of his body up against me and adds a third finger to his ministrations. I bite my lip to swallow the scream bubbling up in my throat. He groans against my neck and finger fucks me to completion. I shift forward and bite his worn lapel, filling my mouth with fabric to muffle the wailing sound of my orgasm—I'm truly putting the ghosts to shame tonight.

"Well now," Al murmurs, kissing my temple with surprising tenderness, "that wasn't too wicked of me, was it?"

I unfurl my fingers from where they've dug themselves into his jacket and lightly slap his chest. He laughs, the sound is like ice skates on a freshly frozen lakes, windchimes dancing on a summer night, eggs frying in a cast iron pan. It's overwhelming, it's disturbingly comforting.

I slowly push him away from me. He lets me maneuver

his body a few steps back. We stare at each other for a moment, the sound of the rain washing away anything that might be left unsaid. I move around him, ducking out from under the boughs of the willow's embrace and head off through the muddy graveyard toward home.

I don't turn around to check if he's following.

I'm no Orpheus.

I know he's there.

CHAPTER 6

THE GHOST WITH THE MOST

his witch walks like a lost soul, a waif, a banshee forever doomed to scream at those who won't heed her warning. A Cassandra through and through. I follow behind her, levitating a few inches off the ground, lurking in her shadow like a plague. She walks with her head held high despite the onslaught of rain. I wanted to get her umbrella for her, but the winds had carried it away. The rain does little to bother me, but I can tell she's cold, her body quivers and shakes the tiniest bit with every step.

We reach the cottage that was once Arletta Harrington's, that strange little witch who vanished into the mist. The idea that a human creature is off in the Realm of the Dead with the Headless Hessian himself is almost too much for even myself to fathom and I've been lurking around these humans since the days when Ichabod Crane was hanged for witchcraft. I've seen many nights pass, countless souls wander through their tiny, meaningless lives, and I've even seen other bodies fall from the ledge of the clocktower.

But never anything like her.

She has an incandescent glow to her unlike these other

breathers with their thoughtless and callous ways. I was created cruel, so to witness beings born good turn to my way of existence is something even a wicked creature like myself finds repulsive.

She's so sad.

So lonely it drips off her in rivulets.

But she's also so alive.

Practically putrid with a passion to exist.

So why did someone with so much life in her ever want to end?

CHAPTER 7

STILL A GOOD WITCH WITH HER TEA

Arletta's house greets me like a tomb.

The air is stale, the stink of incense I burned before work coats the walls, stale coffee sloshing in a discarded mug. I silently grieve Annabel's absence the same as every day, then shuffle to the kitchen and examine the freezer to select a dinner to heat up. I settle on broccoli fettuccine, surely making the ancestors on both sides of my family disappointed in me. I lean against the back counter and pick at my rapidly chipping nail polish while staring at the cardboard dish spin round and round, gathering layers of radiation inside the ancient microwave.

"Got any booze in this place, doll?"

Al materializes in front of me, sitting cross-legged on the counter by the sink. The microwave beeps its pitiful finale. I point to the small wine rack in the corner by the fridge, nothing but a bottle of Pinot Noir left to satisfy him. I don't bother watching him as I take my 'meal' out to cool, but I open the cabinet and retrieve two rarely used wine glasses.

"Can you even drink?" I ask.

He comes up behind me, his front brushing up lightly against my back. I keep my gaze trained on the limp noodles coated in a soupy sauce instead of daring to look at Al.

"I can do a lot of things, babes."

I finally glance at him, taking in his look of disdain over the cheap twist cap. He flicks it off and pours us each a glass, then proceeds to down the latter half of the bottle before roughly plopping it in the sink and picking up his glass.

"Where are you from?" I pick up my dinner and glass of wine and head into the living room, confident that he'll follow. He floats in and settles on the couch beside me. "Like, are you from Hell?"

He chuckles. "Sure."

I sigh. "Can you be serious?"

"No."

"Where do demons come from?"

"Well, when a mommy demon and a daddy demon love each other very much—"

I punch his arm. He laughs louder, a booming, bellowing sound that steals a small smile from my mouth.

"It's a different realm, babes. Different world, hard to even comprehend if this one's the only one you've ever known. You said the dead witch Arletta's with the Horseman? If she's kicking it over in that in-between realm, she might be able to sort of understand the idea of the beyond where I come from."

I huff and take a big gulp of wine. Arletta's shadow blots me out even from beyond the Veil.

"You sore now, doll?" Al teases before throwing back the contents of his glass in one go.

"How can you even drink wine? Isn't this not your real

form? Aren't you just...I don't know, choosing to look like this because my feeble human brain could never fathom your true, supernatural form?"

"Sure. But this form has a stomach, doesn't it?" He plucks my glass from my hand and downs it before I can stop him. "Hard to get drunk, though, I must say. Been trying for what feels like centuries."

"How long have you existed?"

He shrugs. "Long time. Ya gonna stay in those clothes, babes?" My cheeks flush. "Ha! You could, I like how you look wet."

"You're a pervert."

"And you're shivering. You breathers gotta regulate your body temperature, dontcha?"

I finish my sad noodles and get up to toss the cardboard container in the trash. Al follows. I decide to ignore his lewd clothing comments and instead pose another one of the questions about him I've had pounding around in my head since encountering him.

"How are you not being summoned constantly?"

"Hmm?" He quirks a brow.

"Well, if your full name is Albatross how are you not appearing in high school English classrooms across the country every time some kid has to read aloud from *The Rime of The Ancient Mariner?*"

"They gotta say my name three times in a row, which if I recall that poem doesn't do—" *how is he so well versed in classical poetry?* "—and I gotta be summoned with *intent.* They have to know what they're doing when they say it. I ain't no Bloody Mary or Candyman, babycakes."

"Ugh, Al, don't call me *babycakes.*"

He reaches out and playfully cuffs my chin with his fist. "You got it, doll."

We inevitably retreat to my bedroom, the idea of a warm bath and cozy bed is calling to me, but the encroaching presence of Al has my mind flashing with snapshots of my body pressed against the willow while his hands had their way with me.

It was the most alive I've felt in years.

I spin around from my bathroom door to face Al where he's laying on 'his' side of the bed, a book of Adrienne Rich's poetry open before him, his chin resting on one propped up arm. He senses my stare and looks up to meet my gaze.

He pushes the book aside and sits up. "What is it, babes?"

"Do you plan on sticking around? Even if I don't summon you?"

He smirks. "Ain't like I got anywhere else to be. Sick of me already, darlin?"

I press my lips into a thin line. I don't want to give him the satisfaction of admitting that I like his company. He already has too much power over me. I can't help but wonder what he *would* be like at full power. Could he really slay my dragon for me like he said he could?

Al sits up, swinging his legs over the side of the bed to face me.

"I can see the wheels spinning behind your eyes, babes. Care to share with the class what's gotcha all lost in a trance? Or—" he crosses one leg over the other, practically striking a pose, "—is this just you trying to be a scary witch? Cause I gotta say, it's ain't working.

I groan. "No. I'm not trying to be—nevermind. I was just thinking."

"About?"

"How powerful you are."

His eyes flash with a devious kind of glee. "Why? Finally ready to tell me who I gotta kill?"

I shift nervously.

"Don't hold out on me now, babes. Tell me, who had ya wanting to jump."

Same as I did with disclosing to him last night the real reason for Arletta's absence, I decide to share the truth with him once more.

"My older brother. Half-brother. When my parents died I went to live with him, we weren't close; he grew up with his mom—my dad's ex-wife. He's also, like, ten years older than me. So...there was this inherent wall between us. And he...found his own *specific* way to knock it down."

Al stares at me intently, silently for a few moments. I take note of how quickly understanding washes across his eerie gaze. "I see."

"Right, well...um...he moved here several years ago, I thought I was free of him. I couldn't stomach having to see him constantly, so I asked Arletta to make me forget. Herbs are the area of magic where I'm strongest, but the potion wouldn't last forever. Someone had to remind me to take it which means someone needed to be my secret keeper. Someone else needed to hold the weight of the truth. Arletta offered to do it for me. I forgot everything about my brother. I knew he was my brother and we had lived together and weren't close and that was it. I knew there was a potion Arletta reminded me to take and that I had asked her to remind me. I *knew* I had chosen to forget something, and I was perfectly content never to find out what that was. But then..."

"Arletta Harrington left."

I nod, blinking away tears, it seems like all I do lately is cry.

"I have a way to talk to her, at her grave. She kept reminding me. But...I guess it must be hard for her to keep track of time from that world and the potion has to be taken every year at the same time, and...this year she was late. I actually haven't heard from her in months so...one day I woke up and I—" my voice cracks. "I remembered. And I've just...always been so sad. So...dark and insecure. I was a lonely kid, a melancholy teenager, now a cliche adult. Everyone else before Arletta always looked at me in this pitying way like they were basically saying 'hurry up and get happy.' But not everyone's built happy, you know? Arletta embraced my sadness. I was sad, she was angry, it was a good fit. But then she got happy and left me here all alone with my thoughts and my memories and then..." I take a shaky breath. "The day you met me, that morning, I ran into my brother. I looked into his eyes, and it was a tidal wave of pain. My parent's death, Arletta's absence, the awful endless dejection that seems to always lurk in the back of my mind ever since I was a little girl—it all became too much. Too heavy a burden to bear."

An Albatross around my neck.

"So I decided I didn't want to bear it anymore."

Silence settles over me and my Albatross like the ancient mariner's net.

Al stands up and slowly walks over to me. I keep my eyes glued to him. He stops a few feet in front of me and rests his hands on my shoulders. "You can bear it, babes. I know it."

"Maybe," I whisper. I look into his viscous eyes, glowing impossibly green. "Now."

The hint of a smile tugs at the corner of his mouth. He lightly twirls one of my damp curls around his finger. "I'll kill him."

"But...I would have to summon you, right?"

He nods. "Correct. I'm not at full power right now. Don't get me wrong, doll, I could mess with him, but to take a life—remove a human soul from this world—for that I need to be on the loose."

"And then...you'd be free."

He lightly squeezes my shoulders. "But so would you."

I have a minor existential crisis about what my life has become over the course of the past twenty-four hours. I'm finally starting to feel at peace with not dying just yet. Maybe I don't have to be so alone anymore. Still the idea of being responsible for setting a powerful demon loose on the unsuspecting residents of Sleepy Hollow is a heavy burden to bear.

"I don't know," I say.

"Doesn't it haunt you?"

"No, that's your job."

He laughs. I meet his gaze, reach my hand up and gently caress his cheek, he seems to visibly relax into my touch. It's the first touch between us that I've fully initiated.

"Are you a cruel creature, Al?"

He moves one hand from my shoulder to cradle the back of my head. "I'm afraid so, darlin. I'm terribly wicked."

"Hmm."

"You can be wicked too, you know." He leans down and rests his forehead against mine.

I scoff. "The Wicked Witch of the Hollow?"

"Why not?"

I don't respond, I let the silence hang between us, thick as honey.

"Why can I see you?" I breathe.

"I don't know, and I don't care. When I realized you could see me I just knew..." he shrugs, like he can't find the words and doesn't even care that they've vanished in the air. It's remarkable, my bibliophile-self loathes the absence of words.

"Knew what?"

"That you're somebody I can relate to."

"I'm just a sad, lonely girl, Al. I'm nobody."

"Not to me."

I WAKE LATE in the night.

Al is asleep beside me.

How strange that he chooses to do something so unnecessary. I guess it's better than him sitting up and watching me sleep, perched on my chest like The Imp of The Perverse. I roll over to face him, tucking my hands under my cheek.

I have no doubts now.

I don't want to be haunted by anyone or anything ever again, besides him.

"Albatross," I whisper. "Albatross, Albatross."

CHAPTER 8

SINCE WHEN IS BEING A SLUT A CRIME IN THIS FAMILY?

Al's eyes snap open, their green glow more vibrant than I've ever seen them.

A wicked grin spreads across your face, his hands find my hips beneath the blanket, tiny electricity radiating from your fingertips, it makes me gasp so softly.

"Now you've gone and done it, babes."

I hesitate for only a moment before launching myself across the space between us and pressing my mouth to his. He tastes smoky and earthy with a hint of residual red wine left on his lips like a supernova. I part my mouth slightly to let his tongue tangle with mine and fill me with chills. I moan softly and press my body against his. He moves his hands from around my waist to press flat against my back, his large palms spreading across the bare skin my night-gown exposes.

"Samantha," he murmurs.

I tilt my hips against his, savoring the friction the seam of his pants creates against my clit, I know we can both already feel how wet I am.

"Ya positive, babes? I don't need ya hating me in the morning."

I smile against him. "Yeah," I caress his cheek again. "I'm sure."

"Thank fuck for that."

He hooks a hand under my knee and drags me on top of him. I laugh softly as I straddle him, pressing my hips down to elicit a groan from deep in his throat.

"Fucking hell," he says against my skin, trailing kisses along my jaw.

I sit up suddenly, keeping my eyes locked on his fiery ones. I smirk and reach down to grab the hem of my night-gown then pull it over my head and toss it aside, bearing myself completely. Al just stares at me, mouth agape. It's truly something to have the bewitched attention of an otherworldly being just with one's tits. A fucking amazing feeling, actually.

I trail one finger along the waistband of his slacks. "You gonna take these off or leave me hanging here?'

"Say less, babes."

In the blink of an eye Al vanishes all his clothes from his body and onto the floor. Another laugh escapes me. What an absurd use of his power. I look down at his erection pressing up against my stomach and can't help it when my eyes widen. To say he's well hung would be an understate-ment. I'm not a big fan of looking at dicks, they're not really the prettiest thing in my opinion but goddamn if I'm not excited to feel him inside me.

Al smirks, pleased with my reaction. He pinches my hips, causing me to yelp softly.

"Like what ya see, babes?"

He wiggles his hips beneath me, making his admittedly very impressive cock to grind against me.

I lightly slap his chest. "Cocky much?"

He reaches down and takes his length in his hand. "*Yes.*"

I roll my eyes. Al laughs then releases himself to press two fingers against my clit. I jerk in surprise as he begins to apply the perfect amount of pressure, circling methodically, eyes glowing brighter and brighter with every moan that escapes my lips. He brings me to the edge again and again, stopping every time I'm close, chuckling softly when I make soft, frustrated noises. Unable to take it anymore, I smack his hand away, push aside my underwear, and move my hips to line his cock up with my slick entrance. I hesitate, Al digs his fingers into my hips roughly, confusion settling across his brow.

"Darlin, don't tell me after all those pretty, little sounds you're getting cold feet?"

"No, no, no. Just, uh..."

He lightly bucks his hips against me, drawing a laugh free.

"Out with it, doll."

"I can't get pregnant or anything from you, right? This isn't going to turn out like a crazy *Beetlejuice* fanfiction or something?"

"A what?"

"Nevermind. Answer my question."

He smirks. "I'm not alive, babes, I can't make a baby with ya."

"Thank god."

I lift my hips and sink down on top of him. We both moan in tandem, the delicious fullness of his cock filling me up, his girth stretching me wonderfully. I rock my hips against him, his dick hitting the sweet spot inside me that makes me dizzy.

I press my hands on his chest, digging in my nails

slightly in his light trail of chest hair, his hands find my breasts and tug on my nipples, pulling a breathy whimper from my throat.

"That's a pretty sound," he says, his voice so wanton it comes out almost as a growl. "Make it again."

I meet his gaze, a playful, uncharacteristically smug smirk dancing across my face. "Make me, Albatross."

His own lascivious smirk appears. At the same time he thrusts hard into me, hitting that glorious spot again, he tugs hard on my nipples, the tips pebbling beneath his touch. A louder whimper escapes me, and my head falls back, my dark curls spilling down my back. Al shoots up, snakes one arm around me, fingers digging into my back, the other one digs into the hair at the nape of my neck and pulls roughly. I hiss softly from the slightly painful but splendidly sensual feeling the action causes, and rock my hips against him again.

Al shifts forward and suckles at my neck, placing love bites down the column of my throat and along the dip of my collarbone. I whimper and whine so loudly the ghosts in the cemetery must hear me from here. Just when I'm wondering if he possesses the ability to come I feel his body tense against mine, a crescendo clearly building.

"I don't know how much longer I can last, babes. Are you close?"

He tugs my hair again to punctuate his point. I shift up slightly along his shaft and slam myself back down so hard that action alone nearly does me in, and I practically scream. Al chuckles.

"I'll take that as a yes."

We move together, rocking back and forth, wrapped up in each other's sweaty and violent embrace until our dual orgasms wash over us, claiming us both with a supernatural vengeance that makes us cry out in unison into the night.

There's something profoundly powerful in a witch and a demon lying together. I don't know how it didn't occur to me until just now.

Oh, what magic we could make together.

Al falls back on the mattress, taking me with him, our sex-slick bodies making a crude sound as they slap together. I laugh again, euphoric joy unlike anything I've felt in ages simmering through me.

Al smooths down my hair with one hand and presses a gentle kiss to my forehead.

"Good as you hoped?" I ask.

"Babes, this is the best haunting I've ever done.

CHAPTER 9

WHO'S THE BADDEST WITCH IN TOWN?

I wake early on the morning of Samhain and head to my altar. I keep it in the same back room where Arletta did her private magic. I use the cottage to sell my services the same way she did, the only difference being my specialty is green witchcraft whereas Arletta's was always divination.

I kneel before my altar and begin lighting candles. Above the space cluttered with various crystals and tarot cards is an old painting of Perun, the Slovenian God of sky, lightning, thunder, war, and justice. In middle school when I became more invested in my craft is when I first learned about Perun, one of the only Slavic Gods scholars know a wealth about. With many similarities to well-known Pagan deities like Zeus, what truly drew me to him was the final aspect of his power:

Justice.

I retreat to the kitchen to grab an apple. Back at my altar, I hold it before the painting and whisper a soft incantation.

He grabbed three golden apples
And threw them high into the sky
Three lightning bolts burst from the sky
The first struck two young grooms
The second struck Pasho on brown horse
The third struck six hundred wedding
   guests
Not an eyewitness left
Not even to say how they died.

THE APPLE TURNS golden in my palm, a slight glow radiating off the surface. I raise it to my lips and take a juicy bite.

"THIS IS OBNOXIOUSLY CLICHE, BABES."

Al walks into the living room, sporting the same black suit he always wears, just now that he's been summoned it's got a bit more of a spiffy shine to it. The only real change in his attire is on top of his bushy, bright red hair, sits a pair of costume devil horns.

I smirk, adjusting the collar of my dress. "What else was I supposed to dress you up as on such short notice?"

He strides over and quickly swipes at the fake blood I've painted around my mouth. "And all you could come up with for yourself was a sexy vampire?"

"I hadn't intended to be alive for Matilda's Halloween party so I had to work with what I could throw together at the last minute."

"Mmm." He nods and awkwardly looks around the space.

Watching the ghoul look uncomfortable is somewhat hilarious. I start laughing. Al groans dramatically, slides over and wraps his arm around my waist.

"Lead the way, babes."

Matilda always throws a rager on Halloween, and I always find an excuse to opt-out. I never formally decline because it would just lead to her harassing me at work so I always give a loose maybe and text the day of proclaiming some grand reason for my absence. But now that it's actually Halloween and I can't call in dead like I had planned, it's time to step up.

Really we're going because my brother will be there.

In fact, half the town will be in attendance. Folks love to turn out for Matilda's annual spooky shindig. And it's because of this crowd that makes it the perfect location for the slaughter.

Matilda lives in an old Victorian-style manor in the heart of town that looks like it fell out of a Charlotte Brontë novel. The entire place is decked out with Jack-O-Lanterns and orange and purple twinkling lights. The sound of dubstep remixes of classic Halloween songs is blaring from inside, as we pass through the gate at the edge of the lawn I can make out the song currently playing: *Headless Horseman,* how fitting. Nothing like hearing Bing Crosby crooning over a techno beat.

Al leads us up the walkway through the front door, my arm tucked firmly in his, smiling devilishly as he nods at our fellow partygoers. I'm enough of a wallflower in town that no one calls out to me to make a big deal out of my long overdue attendance and I'm grateful. We weave throughout the crowded house, keeping eyes peeled for my brother. After the first lap with no success Al retreats to the kitchen to get us some drinks, and I settle into a corner of the living room to keep an eye out.

"Well, look who it is."

My head snaps to the side to see a tall, blonde man dressed as a zombie football player approaching me.

Ethan.

Arletta's ex.

"The evasive Sam emerges."

Ethan saunters over and leans his arm on the mantle, angling his body towards me, crowding me into a corner, my eyes scan the crowd for Al. I suddenly feel like an idiot for not going with him.

"Hi, Ethan." I want to tell him to fuck off but my anxiety over any form of confrontation wins out. I silently pray to Perun to give me strength; his apple seems to lodge in my throat instead of turning to golden fire in the pit of my belly like I intended. No fierce heroine here, just an eternal Snow White.

There can be great power in quiet, Arletta used to say to me whenever I expressed a desire to be louder and more aggressive like her. *Being gentle and soft doesn't mean you're weak.*

I'm not weak. I can't be. Not anymore. I swallow the proverbial apple in my throat, determined to somehow finally be the hero of my own story. The power of Perun begins to rumble in my gut, begging to be let out. I clench my hands into firsts at my side, hiding the angry knuckles in the folds of my dress, eyes still begging the space for Al to appear. I summoned a demon, I've already shown my strength in such a bold act, a weaker witch would never do what I've done.

I just need to find the damned demon in this awful crowd.

"Hear from Arletta lately?"

"No one hears from her, she's dead." My voice comes out venomous.

Ethan just laughs.

I want to make his teeth crumble in his mouth. With the proper herbs I could turn his cup of cheap jungle juice into a potion that would achieve that very effect. I rifle an unclenched fist in my pocket but only find the protection pouch of herbs I made before leaving. Nothing poisonous to be found inside.

"I heard you've been seen sitting at her grave all alone talking to it. Some folks figure you must be summoning her ghost. Or maybe—" he leans down closer to me, the stink of horribly mixed liquor and store-brand punch heavy on his breath. I have to hold back a gag. "—you're just talking to the voices in your head."

I push off from the wall, launching myself into the crowd to try and escape Ethan. Of course he trails after me, shoving various partygoers out of the way without care.

"Come on, Sam, I'm kidding, take a joke."

I take a turn down a dark hallway further into the manor, Ethan's still in pursuit. I reach the end of the hall, light from the kitchen peeking through the door at the back, I reach for it, muttering Al's full name softly under my breath over and over, far more than three times.

Ethan grabs my elbow, yanking me back and slamming me up against the wall.

"Listen, Sam, everyone knows you and Arletta were close, but I never thought you were a bitch like her."

I raise my hand to slap him, but he catches my wrist

and pins me against the wall, his body slamming into mine so hard it knocks the air out of me.

"Come on, Sam" He leans in close again, his face inches from me. I close my eyes. "Don't you want to have fun?"

Albatross, Albatross, Albatross.

I don't know if I say the words in my head or out loud, my tongue tastes like apples, my fingers glow golden, and I summon my demonic lover to my side with every ounce of power I possess. I'm more than just a party trick green witch. I *am.*

Ethan ignores me, his other hand begins to travel lower when a voice like thunder in the distance speaks from behind him.

"Her name is *Samantha.*"

I open my eyes to see the shadow of Al looming behind Ethan, his eyes glowing a viscous red I've never seen before.

Ethan slowly looks over his shoulder at my demon.

"Who the hell are—"

Before Ethan can finish his sentence Al's hand grabs Ethan's neck, fingers curling around and squeezing until Ethan's face turns purple. Al yanks back, pulling Ethan away from me, his grimy hands falling away from my body. Al slams Ethan up against the opposite wall and lifts him up until his feet dangle off the floor. Ethan desperately scratches at Al's arm, flailing in his hold. I can do nothing but stand still, back glued to the wall, and watch.

"Did you really think you could touch her and get away with it?" Al snarls.

His entire body begins to radiate a shadowy mist that moves and writhes like a living being. Ethan's eyes go wide as saucers, fear dripping from every pore.

"What are you?" he rasps.

Al grins; his teeth have all become razor sharp.

"A nightmare."

I watch the light slowly leave Ethan's eyes, knowing I'm the one who brought this fate before him. I don't know what I thought Al would do, spook him, perhaps. But not this. I never suspect the worst of people, my Achilles heel. I should've reminded myself before we came here that Al isn't human, he isn't my fun new boyfriend, he's an other-worldly being from a dark existence that feeds off destruc-tion. Was I really so lonely and sad that some good demon dick blinded me to the dangers I was about to unleash on Sleepy Hollow?

On Samhain no less?

Arletta would be chiding me for being so fucking stupid if she were here.

But she's not here. She's off fucking a death being of her own.

She was stupid wandering off into the woods in nothing but a nightgown that Halloween night that feels so long ago. I guess it was my turn to tamper with the unknown, the occult more powerful than even she or I could ever be.

So it's up to me to reign this creature in.

I lightly squeeze his arm.

"Al," I say again. "You can stop now."

Al's hand on Ethan's throat twitches, it's clear Ethan only has moments left. I fear tears prick my lashes, I suddenly don't know if I can be responsible for Ethan's death. Or my brother's. Or anyone's.

Al decides for me.

He snaps Ethan's neck with an ugly crack, and then Ethan's body slinks to the floor in a heap of drunken dead limbs. My hands go to my mouth, covering it hard, gagging myself to stifle my scream as I witness a swift and nearly silent murder. Al props him against the wall, making it look to any passerby like he's just had too much to drink.

Al turns to face me. The burning demon is gone, leaving with the same breath as Ethan's life. *My* Albatross stands before me but my stomach churns. I'm going to be sick. I turn and race through the kitchen and outside where I heave over and vomit onto the lawn. No one pays me any mind, throwing up at Matilda's Halloween rager is nothing out of the ordinary to these people.

I feel Al's hand on my back, I flinch slightly from the touch.

"I've seen that guy around before," Al says, ignoring my flinch. "He messed with your witch friend. Arletta."

I stand up straight and turn around. "He did. He hurt her. A lot."

Al glances out at the guests scattered across the lawn beneath the twinkling lights strung through the trees. "Take it these breathers didn't care?" I shake my head. "Guess it's doubly good I took care of it then, huh?"

"You're a demon, not a vigilante," I insist.

"You invited me here tonight to kill someone, babes."

"Not Ethan."

Al shrugs. "What does it matter? You really think that scum deserved to live?"

"Do *you*?"

Al chuckles, materializing a cigarette between his fingers. "I'm dead, doll."

"Ugh, fuck you!"

I turn and storm away, up onto the wrap around porch, walking off to the side of the house where the outdoor lamps leave the space in shadows. Al follows me.

"Babes, look, he was trying to—"

"I know what he was trying to do but you just—"

Al vanishes his barely smoked cigarette and grabs my arms, holding me still; not hard enough to hurt, but still.

"I know what I did, and you know what I am. You knew it when you summoned me so don't go feeling bad about it now. You really think Arletta Harrington throws a fit when the Horseman kills people?"

"I...that's not the same."

"Ain't it?"

He's right. It is. I can't be mad at him for being what he is.

"Babes," he says again, sweeter this time. He moves one hand to cradle the back of my head. "It'll be fine. Trust me."

"Trusting you is stupid."

"But you do it anyway."

I press my hands to his chest, but I don't shove him away, just lightly—almost playfully—slap him. "Yeah, well."

Al pulls my face in close and kisses me hard; my fake vampire blood smearing across his smoky mouth. I whimper soft and kiss him back, gripping the lapels of his suit, pulling his body flush against mine. He wastes no time in tugging up my dress and sliding his hand between my legs. I hear him inhale sharply when he realizes I'm not wearing any panties. I smirk against his mouth and tilt my pelvis against his palm.

"Fucking Hell, babes."

"That's the idea."

He thrusts three fingers inside me, using his other hand to clamp down over my mouth and stifle my screams as he starts finger fucking me ferociously without bothering to build up any momentum, just diving right in, flooring it through the fences of my apprehension. I moan against his palm, my hands gripping his coat, legs shaking as he hits the sweet spot against my inner wall over and over again, fingers curling perfectly against me until a quick and sticky climax drips from between my legs.

I'm going straight to hell. Guess I'll see Arletta and Hesse there.

We spot my brother in the crowd a little while later, we've been lurking in the shadows of the porch chain-smoking Al's mysterious cigarettes.

"There he is," I whisper, spotting a tall white guy dressed in a half-assed Superman costume (a Superman t-shirt and jeans) waltz across the backyard to where Matilda is standing around an outdoor bar.

"What's his name?" Al asks.

"Peyton."

"Disgusting."

I nod. "Entirely."

Al looks at me; I meet his gaze, staring into his shining eyes across the dark.

"You ready, babes? Ya ain't gonna go soft on me after, are ya?"

I shake my head, resolute. "Not at all."

Al grins. "Alright then, it's showtime."

Al makes himself invisible, something he can control with his powers at full capacity. I lurk in the shadows of the tree line, watching as the ghoul only I can see stalks my half-brother around the yard and into the house. He promised to make it a long, thorough, bloody death. I eagerly await the screams.

They immediately draw the attention of the crowd outside. People drop drinks to the ground, let the grass extinguish their cigarettes as they run drunkenly in cheap costumes towards the house. I slide away into the woods to await the darkness.

For a split second I could swear Matilda glances over her shoulder and meets my eye.

But how could she? No one can see through shadows this thick.

She hesitates for only a moment, then takes off after her guests to uncover my brother's corpse. I hope it's bloody. I hope it traumatizes. I hope everyone remembers what it looks like—what happens when you hurt a witch.

CHAPTER 10

HE DOES NOT WORK WELL WITH OTHERS

It's been so long since I've tasted such sweet screams.

It's so wonderful to watch the wretch writhe on the bathroom floor as I rip his soul apart.

I think of Samantha's face, the peace that will be brought to her beautiful eyes once this nightmare is gone from the world.

The only monster she needs is me.

CHAPTER II

YOU HAD THE POWER WITHIN YOU ALL ALONG, MY DEAR

I'm sitting by Arletta's grave, Samhain night well underway, no sightings of the Headless Horseman to report, and Peyton and Ethan long since dead.

I feel somewhat hollow inside as I wait for guilt or agony or…something to sink in. No such emotions come. I heard sirens in the distance as I made my way to the cemetery. No one paid me any mind as I lurked through the streets. Just another ghost.

"I miss you, Arletta." I trace the letters of her name, willing the portal to open, silently begging her to come.

I sense Al without having to look up at him.

He settles down beside me in the grass, already damp with early morning dew. His smoky, earthy scent is mixed with the lingering stain of cheap booze and potent weed from Matilda's house. I never even got a chance to say hi to Matilda before I let my demon commit double homicide.

Al's hand reaches out and finds mine across the small sea of grass. He weaves our fingers together against the darkness.

"Samantha."

My heart nearly explodes.

My eyes water, blurring my vision of Arletta's name.

Al squeezes my fingers. "I love you. You know that, right?"

I finally turn to look at him, glowing green finding me in the dead of night.

"Yes," I breathe. "I know."

CHAPTER 12

I'M A WITCH, I CAN'T JUST NOT BE

1 YEAR LATER

Matilda drops a box of books on the front counter, nearly knocking over my coffee. I scramble to save my to-go cup before peering over the edge of the box. Inside sits stacks upon stacks of some new, shiny hardback thriller penned by some vaguely familiar male author.

"We got three dozen pre-orders for this," Matilda explains.

I sip my coffee. "And it's releasing today? It's Halloween." I reach in and tap a book. "New releases come out on Tuesdays, not Fridays."

"I know. It does come out Tuesday, I guess the publisher was hoping to appeal to the year-round Halloween lovers, but I figured we could sneak a few on the shelves early."

"Matilda," I mock chide, "you bad girl."

"Hey—" she holds her hands up in fake surrender. "—if Target can do it, so can we."

I laugh, push my coffee aside, and reach into the box plucking a few books out. I descend into the stacks without further direction from Matilda.

"What is this trash?" Al plucks a book from the top of the stack as I pass him by.

He likes to make himself invisible and pop out around the bookstore on days when I have long shifts. The first few weeks it always startled me, but I soon became well attuned to his presence. He used to lurk around Sleepy Hollow, preying on unsuspecting townspeople but I put an end to that. I'm sure he still gets up to his mischief from time to time but at least during the work week I tend to have a pretty good handle on him.

We've had a good year together. Spending the nights tangled up in my sheets. Sometimes we watch scary movies together, or Al endures one of the regency romance films I love, and I pretend to be offended when he makes jabs at Mr. Darcy. I still visit Arletta's grave and the portal still remains silent. I pray to Perun. I'm still somewhat plagued with thoughts of death. And Ethan and Peyton's murders were never solved. I wasn't even a suspect. But their two odd deaths coupled with Arletta's disappearance gave the internet the fuel it needed for a new paranormal true crime craze. There's currently three active podcasts about the ordeal. Matilda listens to *Tales from the Headless* every Friday. It's co-hosted by two obnoxious men who claim that they're 'real-life vampires.' I don't know how she can tolerate such trash. Luckily today I'm spared from the true crime trash and blessed with one of Matilda's playlists; this one is very Kate Bush heavy.

I take the book back from Al, making my way to the horror section. "I don't know. The kind of book that sells well in airports."

Al floats along beside me, lounging out horizontally as if he's lying on a beach towel. "They sell books in airports?"

I begin shelving. "Mmhm. They sell pretty much everything in airports nowadays, they're like cities." I look up at him, he waggles his eyebrows. "No." I hold a finger up to him like I'm scolding a dog. "I am not letting you loose in an airport."

"You're no fun, doll."

When I finish shelving the sneaky release I make my way back to the front, the shop has cleared out of customers, most people heading home to prepare for trick-or-treating and parties. Matilda is sitting on a stool behind the cash register, black nails tip-tapping against her mug of tea. She looks at me curiously as I approach.

"What?" I laugh awkwardly.

"Nothing." She smiles and sets down her mug. She wipes away a stray drop of tea from the corner of her mouth. I watch, confused, as her finger comes away stained red. "I'm just wondering when you're going to finally explain to me why the demon that killed Ethan and Peyton at my Halloween party last year is following you around all the time."

I nearly drop dead.

Al materializes beside me, laughing hysterically.

"Guess the cat's out of the bag. What'd ya know, doll?" Al elbows me gently in the side, I shove him away, eyes still trained on Matilda. "Are you a witch too?" he asks my boss.

Matilda laughs.

Then she parts her blood-red lips and exposes her teeth. I don't understand at first what she's doing but then I have to stifle a yelp of shock when fangs begin to protrude from where her canine teeth should be. It's as if her normal—*human*—teeth were simply just a trick of the light. She now sits before me, a true creature of the night. I glance at her tea mug again.

Her red-stained finger.

I've never seen her eat anything.

Her endless umbrellas, even when it's sunny.

"Lord almighty, Matilda," I say.

She laughs again. "Oh, Samantha, there's so much you don't know about the Hollow."

Matilda closes early and we open a bottle of wine.

Well, I do. She has her...tea. We curl up on the couch in the classics section as the night carries on around us, The Veil growing thinner by the minute. I have so many questions, but I don't get a chance to ask any of them because she goes right ahead asking about Al, who I sent home to keep out of trouble, but honestly I'm sure he's already lurking the streets, scaring trick or treaters.

"So why did you summon a demon?"

I swish my glass of wine around, making a whirlpool out of the beverage. "Because he asked."

"Come on."

I look up at her, trying not to stare at the fangs poking out around her lips. "Matilda, you're my boss, I don't think it's appropriate to dump my personal trauma on you."

"Samantha, honey—" she leans back against the couch. "—who else are you going to talk to about it? Face it, we've got to stick together; you're a witch, I'm a vampire, you're dating a demon, and don't even get me started on your girl, Arletta."

"You know about Arletta?"

She drinks some of her *tea*. "Mmhmm. Saw them riding

by last Halloween. She looked good. Ridiculous and kind of slutty, like if Elvira and Goody Proctor had a baby, but good, nonetheless. So, yeah, I know she isn't dead. Just like I know a smart girl like you has a good reason for bringing a demon into our midst."

"I didn't *bring* him here. He already *was* here."

She points a sharp nail at me. "But he wasn't free."

I down half my glass. "I just...I started feeling so sad all the time at such a young age and then it's like that's all I was. How was I supposed to escape it? Because if I'm not my depression, then who am I? But people don't love sad girls. They look right past us, pray we won't become those angry sad girls, and god forbid you try to explain why you're angry, then they'll really hate you." Matilda parts her bloody lips to respond but I don't let her. "People—*men*—hate rape survivors. Sure, they can pretend they're an advocate in theory until they come face to face with someone who requires them to exert an iota of emotional intelligence. I swear, so many of them must think they can just fuck you good enough and it'll erase it all, but don't get it twisted, they don't want to erase it so that *you* feel better but rather so they don't have to be careful anymore."

"And so...I've just been...aching with this loneliness and there he was, so willing to take it all away. I don't think I even fully stopped to question the sanity of trusting him—I just did. Maybe that's incredibly stupid of me, but Matilda, when I'm with him being a sad girl doesn't feel like a weakness anymore. When I'm with him...I feel like myself again."

Matilda studies me intently for a moment, then finally raises her mug in the air. "Cheers to that."

We clink glasses.

She doesn't ask me why he killed Ethan and Peyton. She's too wise a woman for that.

A blessed Samhain to all.

~

AL PRACTICALLY TACKLES me when I walk through the door. His mouth finds mine immediately as his hands pin my wrists to the door. I'm as hungry for him as he is for me, so I eagerly part my legs and let him grind himself up against me.

"You got any customers lined up tonight, babes?" he rasps into my ear before nipping at the lobe.

"No. I don't do that shit on Samhain. Tonight's for me." Al shifts to look me in the eye. I grin. "For us."

"Thank fuck."

He sweeps me up into his arms and carries me to the bedroom, practically tossing me onto the mattress with a bounce. I start to undo the laces of my dress, but he uses his powers to discard our clothes to the floor. I squeal in surprise as the chilly October air assaults my bare skin without any warning.

"Aren't you a pretty sight." He crawls on top of me, sliding a hand between us to press against my cunt, already wet for him. "Fucking hell, babes."

I wrap my hands around his neck, pulling his mouth down to mine. He takes my bottom lip between his teeth and bites down so hard I cry out, the sound getting lost in his sweet, smokey mouth. He slides two fingers inside me, crooking them forward to make me croon, my back bowing against the mattress beneath me.

"Stop teasing, Albatross."

His body tenses slightly, hearing his full name always undoes him, even a year after being properly summoned. I suppose theoretically I could figure out how to put him back, re-tether him to the confines of the other plane of existence he was on before I set him free. But I don't want to.

"Oh, babes." He kisses the hollow of my throat. "Say less."

He removes his fingers and replaces them with his cock, slamming into me fast and hard. I grip his red hair and tug so hard a few strands come out, a strangled, pitiful sound escaping my throat as he pounds into me, fucking me to hell and back.

What a wicked pair we make.

"Samantha," he murmurs into my hair as his hips piston against mine.

In the same way that I rarely say Albatross, he rarely says Samantha. Our true names are keys to the secret gardens of our hearts. They unlock wonders inside that no one else can ever truly understand.

I sigh happily, nipping at his shoulder, savoring the salty taste of his skin. He groans and his hands make their way to my breasts, he tugs on my nipples hard the way he knows I like. I whimper louder and louder as he moves his fingers with deft precision to inflict beautiful torture upon my chest. My whimpers soon turn to inhumane sounds of pleasure and desire. He keeps fucking me relentlessly until we can both feel our peak building together. I dig my nails into his back and he wraps a hand around my throat. I gasp as my vision blurs, his other hand reaches down between us and his fingers start to rapidly circle my clit. It's such a beautiful onslaught of numerous sensations that I can barely keep my thoughts straight.

Al moans loudly, his head falls forward into the crook of my neck, and he bites down hard on the juncture between my shoulder blade and the column of my throat.

We finish with a scream like an incantation.

Al collapses down beside me, taking me into his arms. I nuzzle against his chest, feeling safe and protected.

"Hey," I whisper.

"Hmm?"

"I love you too."

He chuckles softly. "Took you a year to say it and the first time you say it is in bed? Well, ain't you classy."

I playfully slap his cheek. "Fuck off, demon, I'll take it back. The power of Christ compels you and all that."

"Oh, does it? Does it compel me?"

He tackles me with a kiss, and I can already feel the energy shift into one of wanton passion again. One of the perks of dating a demon is there isn't a very long wait time in between erections.

I climb on top of him, straddling him with my hips, already imagining him sinking his teeth deep into my flesh as I come, but then there's a knock at the door. We both freeze.

"Thought you said you don't have any customers?"

I shake my head. "I don't."

I clamber off the bed, grab my dress and do my best to tug it on, the laces half undone as I make my way to the front door. I open it and feel my soul leave my body when I see who's standing on my front porch.

"Hi," Arletta Harrington says with a goddamn smile. "Sorry I'm late."

ACKNOWLEDGMENTS

Thank you to the people who helped make this book happen:

Jay Gaunt and Marcia Ruiz-Olguín for being my steadfast supporters, brilliant early readers, providing fundamental edits and valuable critiques. For being guiding lights and giving vital emotional support to me all these years. My life and my writing is better because of you two.

Naeemkhan for saving me from my complete bumbling, inability to format a paperback cover to save my life. You make the process such a breeze and it's such a relief to have you onboard.

Karolyn Haines aka palatte_priestess on instagram for stepping in to create this beautiful cover. I know it was a step outside of your usual style to make something that would match the vibes of Arletta and Hesse on book 1's cover but you went above and beyond my expectations with your lovely art. You truly brought Samantha and Al to life.

My sister Katy for repeatedly saying "You could make it a series! Like the Sookie Stackhouse books!" I was convinced for over a year that there simply wasn't any more story to be told in my sexy version of Sleepy Hollow and you helped me see otherwise.

My hype team: Ali, Fern, Mika, and Amanda Nikole, for making promotion and marketing so much simpler, and your support is forever invigorating.

All of the BookTokers, Bookstagrammers, and readers who kept asking for this story to continue. Your continued faith in the silly, campy, spicy story of Riding The Headless Horseman made this possible.

My mom. For everything. Absolutely everything. I don't even have the words to fully encapsulate how immense and important you've been over the course of my writing journey from when I was 6 years old to today. Ly3.

Prancer and Wendy for watching over me, and to Edgar and Lizzy for stepping in to walk beside me when Prancer and Wendy no longer could.

Washington Irving. I'm so sorry for taking your literary masterpiece and turning it into smut, but it simply had to be done.

Arletta and Hesse. You are the most present fictional characters I've ever created, you haunt my life in the most wonderful way. I hope you stay alive in my mind and in readers' hearts, always.

And lastly...thank you to Beetlejuice. Beetlejuice. Beetlejuice. You all know why ;)

ABOUT THE AUTHOR

Molly Likovich is the #1 Amazon Bestselling Author of *Riding The Headless Horseman*. Her writing has appeared in numerous literary magazines and anthologies including *Rust + Moth, The New Mexico Review,* and *Love Letters to Poe Vol. 3.* She has a B.A. in Creative Writing and considers herself an unof!cial Beetlejuice Scholar. When she's not writing she can be found haunting the nearest cemetery or re-watching classic Barbie !lms. Learn more at molly-likovich.com and follow her on TikTok, Instagram & YouTube @magicalmolly

Also by Molly Lilkovich

SEXY SLEEPY HOLLOW SERIES

Riding The Headless Horseman (#1)

Smashing Pumpkins (#1.5)

Romanced by The Headless Horseman (#1.75)

Getting With The Ghoul (#2)

THE FAOINSGEUL WOODS DUET

Not a Myth (#1)

The Willow's Silence (#2)

STAND-ALONES

Send in The Clowns

There's Something in The Woods

Loved Alone

Be Terrible

Falling for Jack Frost

The Firefighter Before Christmas

FANFICTION

Lumos & Lattes (Dramione)

www.ingramcontent.com/pod-product-compliance
Lightning Source LLC
Chambersburg PA
CBHW060506300726
48975CB00008B/2673